GREENDALE

Come and say hello to Julian Clifton!

Postman Pat's son loves to swap cards and letters with his best friend, Meera, and the rest of the gang at Greendale Primary. But when it's time to send party invitations, he decides to make something really special...

"Now click 'go' and you're there," said Julian. He was giving his dad a computer lesson.

"I've surfed the Internet at last!" chuckled Pat, as Sara walked in with a tray of tea and toast.

"Do you want to learn about email now, Dad?"

Sara shook her head. "You've got those invitations to do remember?"

"Thanks, Mum," said Julian. "I'd better start work."

Julian was throwing a party to celebrate the end of term. His mum was going to make a big cake and his dad was planning some brilliant games.

"I'm going to design a special invitation for each of my friends," Julian explained to Pat later.

"I bet they'll look terrific!" said Pat.

"I'll finish them off tomorrow," said Julian, excitedly. "Can't wait to send them out!"

"Thank you, Lucy, that's very interesting," said Jeff Pringle in school on Friday. "Does anyone else have any news?"

Julian's hand shot up. "I do! I've organised a surprise for everyone before we break up for the holidays."

"What? Tell us!" the whole class shouted at once.

"Just keep Sunday free," beamed Julian. "And look out for the post..."

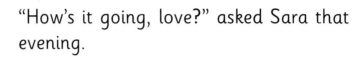

"How's it going, love?" asked Sara that evening.

"I've just got to print the invitations out now, Mum," said Julian.

"Fantastic! I'll fetch some envelopes."

"Miaow!" Jess hopped onto the desk to take a closer look.

Julian gave him a friendly stroke. "Hey, mind the keyboard... ooh!!!'

It was too late. Jess had knocked the 'off' button with his paw.

"I hadn't pressed 'save'!" gulped Julian.

All the invitations had disappeared.

"I'll help you redo them, son," said Pat.

Julian shook his head. "We'll never get them finished tonight, and I'll miss the late post."

Jess gulped, did that mean the party was cancelled?

Pat wasn't going to give up that easily. "Switch the computer on again, Julian."

"Why?"

"There's still an hour 'til bedtime," Pat explained. "If we work as a team we can get the invites done."

The whole family joined in. Pat printed out some pictures onto card, then Sara added glitter and Julian wrote a message inside. Even Jess licked the envelopes.

First thing the next morning, Julian, Pat and Jess made their own special Saturday delivery round.

Knock! Knock!

"Hello, Julian," grinned Meera, opening her front door. "What are you up to?"

Julian handed her an invite. "Can you come to my end-of-term party?"

"Cool! That sounds ace!"

Charlie Pringle's house was next...

Bill Thompson was the last name on the list.

"Wow! Thanks, Julian!" he shouted, tearing open the envelope. "Can't wait!"

"Time to go home then," smiled Pat. "We've got a party to get ready."

Jess leapt up into Julian's arms and started to purr happily.

"I'm so chuffed everyone can make it, Dad!"

The party was a success. There were balloons, lots of games and a fantastic party spread.

"Time to cut the cake, Julian," said Sara.

"One second, Mrs Clifton," said Tom Pottage, pulling out a giant card.

"We wanted to say thanks to Julian for working so hard!" Meera explained.

Julian beamed at his mum and dad. "It was worth every minute!"

SIMON AND SCHUSTER
First published in 2006 in Great Britain by Simon & Schuster UK Ltd.
Africa House, 64-78 Kingsway, London WC2B 6AH

ISBN 1416910611
EAN 9781416910619
Printed in China
1 3 5 7 9 10 8 6 4 2